The Tumbleweed Christmas Tree

Story by Bridget Thomas

Illustrations by Jessie Baca

One cold December, not too long ago, Molly noticed big tumbleweeds blowing across the streets in her hometown of Santa Fe, New Mexico. Anytime she and her mother were in the car to go to the supermarket, the post office, or the library, Molly would see at least one or two tumbleweeds rolling down the road. In all of her seven years, she had never seen so many tumbleweeds!

Santa Fe is considered a desert, but Molly never thought of it as one. When she thought of deserts, she imagined endless stretches of beige, sandy dunes, and bellowing camels tromping across the landscape. Since there weren't any camels in Santa Fe, nor sandy dunes, she'd never really believed that it was a desert. Usually there was plenty of snow on the ground by the first of December, but this year, no snow. No snow and lots of tumbleweeds. The idea of Santa Fe being a desert seemed a bit more real.

Molly was excited about Christmas. Even though there was no snow, it was still very cold, and at night Molly could smell the delicious aroma of piñon fires that filled her neighborhood. Piñon is the Spanish word for pine. Mrs. Lopez, her second grade teacher, had taught the class that last week.

8

Already the hotels, restaurants, and shops had begun to decorate with plastic farolitos. Real farolitos were better of course. Molly loved to pour sand into brown paper lunch sacks, place the small, white novena candles inside, and have her mother light them on Christmas Eve. But real farolitos were too much work to do every day, all month long, so the businesses usually just put up the plastic kind. Even the plastic ones made the city look special, and put people in the Christmas spirit.

Molly and her mother didn't have a tree yet. The Aragons already had their tree. In fact, most of the other families on the block had their trees up and decorated. Molly could see the lights shining through the windows when she and her mother took their nightly walks around the neighborhood to smell the piñon fires and look at the stars.

Molly figured it would just be a matter of time before they went to Noelancy's Christmas tree lot and picked out a tree. Everyday they drove past the lot on the way home, and everyday Molly thought they might stop, but her mother kept her eyes straight ahead and drove on past.

Finally, about a week before Christmas, Molly's mother sat her down to talk about buying a tree.

"Molly, Honey, I know you've been wondering why we haven't bought a tree yet, but this year we just can't afford one. The nicest trees are around $100, and even the scraggly ones are nearly $40. Also, when we moved, I lost the box of ornaments we've had for so long. We would have to spend at least another $30 or $40 on enough decorations to make it look pretty. I'm sorry, Sweetie. Next year we can get a tree for sure."

"That's OK. I don't mind," Molly said.

"You're sure?" her mother asked. Molly nodded. "Thanks, Honey. I love you so much."

"I love you too, Mommy."

The news about the Christmas tree didn't make Molly feel sad or disappointed; she truly didn't mind. The teachers at Holy Faith School had always said that Christmas wasn't really about trees and decorations. It was about celebrating Jesus' birthday and experiencing God's presence within us, not just the presents under the tree.

Suddenly, Molly had a great thought.

"Maybe that's why there are so many tumbleweeds this year! God knew we wouldn't have enough money for a tree, so He gave us tumbleweeds."

"What are you talking about?" her mother asked.

"We can go find two tumbleweeds, pile one on top of the other, buy a string of fairy lights, I saw them on sale at Ortega's for only $2.99, and some little gold balls, and decorate our tumbleweed tree with those. I bet the lights and the balls would cost us less than $7 altogether. Can we afford $7?" Molly asked.

"Yes, I think we can manage that," her mother said with a huge smile.

So, Molly and her mother set out to find the perfect tumbleweeds. They saw a few that were too big, a few that were too small, soon they found two that were just right. They piled the tumbleweeds into the trunk of the car and headed off to Ortega's Emporium. They bought a string of lights, a box of gold balls, and even had enough left over for a little paper angel which was on sale for 99¢. She had a little stamp on the back of her dress that said, "Hecho en Mexico," and she was perfect for the top of the tumbleweed tree.

Once home, Molly and her mother cleaned up an empty clay pot that had been in the yard and put the tumbleweeds on top. They decorated them with the lights, the gold balls, and finally the angel from Mexico. They drew the curtains and plugged in their creation.

The tumbleweed Christmas tree was beautiful, and the little paper angel glowed like she was in heaven. Molly felt a glow in her heart and knew that a whole host of real angels was standing beside them enjoying the tumbleweed Christmas tree as well.

Bridget Thomas grew up in Santa Fe, New Mexico. As a child, she ran around the plaza, splashed in the Santa Fe River, and enjoyed making farolitos at Christmas. One year, she and her mother made the tumbleweed Christmas tree on which this story is based. After a 20 year absence, during which she lived primarily in Colorado, Japan, and California, Bridget returned to the beautiful, funky, Land of Enchantment where she now lives with her family in a small town near Santa Fe.

Jessie Baca resides in Santa Fe, New Mexico with her son, Jay. She grew up in sunny California where she studied fine art and art history in Los Angeles. As the daughter of two artists, she has been drawing and crafting for as long as she can remember. Living in New Mexico brings much inspiration to her through rich color palettes and exquisite textiles and she is happy to call such an enchanted place, "home."

Made in the USA
Columbia, SC
17 December 2024

49972451R00018